THE LOVE THAT NEVER CEASED

SOMETIMES LOVE WALKS AWAY

AF647750

ROHAN BROWNE

BlueRose ONE
Stories Matter
New Delhi • London

BLUEROSE PUBLISHERS
India | U.K.

BlueRose ONE
Stories Matter
New Delhi • London

For permissions requests or inquiries regarding this publication, please contact:

BLUEROSE PUBLISHERS
www.BlueRoseONE.com
info@bluerosepublishers.com
+91 8882 898 898
+4407342408967

ISBN: 978-93-6261-339-4

Cover Design: Sadhna Kumari
Typesetting: Pooja Sharma

First Edition: June 2024

Contents

Chapter 1

A Twofold Loss

The scorching heat of a sweltering August afternoon engulfed Jhansi, casting a heavy haze over the town. Ishan found himself seeking solace indoors, desperate to escape both the relentless sun and the grief that consumed him. It had only been a few days since he had tearfully bid farewell to his beloved mother.

In the quiet solitude of his room, Ishan grappled with the weight of his loss. His mother's comforting presence and soothing words were now just memories. Her absence left him feeling untethered, adrift in a sea of anguish.

Ishan: (whispering to himself) "Mom, I miss you so much."

As he retraced the steps of his mother's final days, Ishan found solace in the whispers of Jhansi. The town's gentle rustling leaves and the soft hum of the wind seemed to carry his mother's spirit, offering a fleeting sense of connection and peace.

Ishan: (whispering to the wind) "Mom, are you still with me?"

In the depths of his grief, Ishan realized that the pain he carried was twofold. The loss of his mother had left an irreparable void in his life. And now, the departure of Varuni, his closest confidante, added another layer of heartache.

Ishan: (voice quivering) "Varuni, why did you leave when I needed you the most?"

Jhansi became a mirror to Ishan's emotional landscape, reflecting the depths of his pain. Yet, it also offered a glimmer of hope for healing, a place where he could find solace amidst the turmoil within.

In the solitude of his room, Ishan sought solace in the memories of his mother's love.

Ishan: (softly, to a framed photo of his mother) "I'll make you proud, Mom. I promise."

It was through the legacy of her love that Ishan found the strength to face the sudden departure of Varuni. He knew that the resilience instilled in him by his mother would guide him through life's storms.

As the sun set on that fateful August afternoon, Ishan carried the weight of his twofold loss, his heart heavy with grief and longing.

Ishan: (looking out the window) "I'll find my way through this darkness, one step at a time."

Jhansi, with its whispered echoes and timeless beauty, would serve as a constant reminder of the love he had lost and the strength he would need to forge ahead.

Chapter 2

A Summer Encounter

July enveloped Jhansi in its warm embrace, marking the beginning of a new chapter in Ishan's life. Fresh out of 12th grade, he longed for the thrill of college life and new experiences. While many of his friends scattered to distant cities for their higher education, Ishan's parents, eager to keep him close, encouraged him to attend the local town college.

Ishan's Parents: (encouraging) "You'll do well here, Ishan. It's a good opportunity."

Respecting his parents' wishes, Ishan embraced the chance to explore the familiar surroundings he had known all his life. He delved into the college admissions process, tackling the paperwork and formalities with a mix of excitement and nervousness. When that acceptance letter from the local town college arrived, relief and anticipation washed over him.

The college campus, nestled amidst Jhansi' picturesque landscapes, greeted Ishan with open arms. Sun-kissed pathways and vibrant greenery hinted at the promise of growth and new beginnings. As he stepped onto the campus, a whirlwind of emotions stirred within him—eagerness, curiosity, and a touch of apprehension.

In the bustling corridors and lively classrooms, Ishan was surrounded by a diverse array of fellow students. Conversations buzzed around him, filled with ideas and the collective pursuit of knowledge. While some of his friends were far away, Ishan discovered the beauty of making new connections and broadening his horizons right here in Jhansi.

Ishan: (thinking) "It's time to step out of my comfort zone."

However, there was a twist. His entire school life had been in an all-boys school, leaving him with lingering shyness when it came to talking to girls.

Ishan: (nervously) "I've got to change that."

Within the bustling college corridors, Ishan's gaze landed on Varuni, a fellow student who stood out from the crowd. Her deep complexion and the charming mole on her chin made her uniquely striking. The moment Ishan laid eyes on her; a spark of curiosity ignited within him. He found himself captivated by her presence, every smile and movement etching itself into his memory.

Ishan: (to himself) "Who is she? I need to know."

Yet, Ishan's shyness and inexperience in interacting with girls held him back. He admired Varuni from afar

, secretly yearning for the opportunity to get to know her better. Jhansi became both a haven and a challenge, offering numerous opportunities for their paths to cross, but Ishan's hesitation kept him at a distance.

In lecture halls and campus gardens, Ishan observed Varuni from afar, his heart quickening with each fleeting glance they shared. He wondered if she noticed him, if she felt the same unspoken connection he did. Jhansi, with its serene beauty and its whispered echoes, bore witness to Ishan's internal struggle—a delicate dance between desire and self-doubt.

Weeks turned into months, and Ishan's infatuation deepened. Jhansi, with its tranquil charm, was the backdrop to his silent yearning. His heart grappled with the desire to step out of his comfort zone, but the fear of rejection held him back. He sought reassurance from the gentle breeze that whispered encouragement in familiar corners of the town.

Then, one day, as Ishan mustered the courage to approach Varuni, he found himself standing before her, his voice caught in his throat. In that fleeting moment, their eyes locked, and a knowing smile graced Varuni's lip. It was as if she had sensed Ishan's silent admiration, his unspoken words of affection. In that moment, a bridge of unspoken understanding was formed between them.

Varuni: (smiling warmly) "Hi, Ishan."

Their silent connection became a catalyst for change. Ishan's shyness gradually melted away, replaced by newfound boldness. Jhansi became the stage for their unspoken dialogue, where every corner held the potential for shared conversations and stolen moments of connection.

As the days passed, Ishan and Varuni grew comfortable in each other's silent presence. They navigated the college corridors together, their gazes speaking volumes, and their smiles bridging the silence between them. Jhansi, with its timeless charm, was the canvas for their silent courtship, a delicate dance of unspoken affection.

And so, as summer transformed into the vibrant hues of autumn, Ishan's admiration for Varuni deepened, his heart expanding with the hope of a connection yet to be fully realized. Jhansi, with its whispered echoes and its ability to inspire courage, held the promise of a future where their unspoken bond might finally find its voice.

Chapter 3

A December Proposal

As the days turned into weeks, Ishan's silent admiration for Varuni slowly began to blossom into a connection that transcended their unspoken words.

Ishan: (smiling) "Varuni, did you catch the movie last night?"

Varuni: (grinning) "Yeah, it was fantastic! I loved that twist at the end."

Jhansi, with its timeless charm, witnessed their growing bond as they gradually started to talk, breaking through the barriers of shyness and uncertainty.

Conversations between Ishan and Varuni flowed effortlessly, each exchange deepening their understanding of one another.

Ishan: "You know, Varuni, I've always wanted to learn how to play the guitar."

Varuni: "Really? I play. I could give you some lessons."

They discovered shared interests, laughed at each other's jokes, and found solace in the comfort of their companionship.

Jhansi, with its serene landscapes and whispered echoes, became the backdrop of their budding relationship—a sanctuary where their love could flourish.

As the year ended, a new thought took hold of Ishan's heart—an idea that filled him with excitement and nervous anticipation. He decided that on the magical evening of December 24th, he would gather the courage to propose to Varuni, expressing the depth of his feelings and his desire to embark on a lifelong journey by her side.

Ishan: (to himself) "This is it, the perfect moment."

With each passing day, Ishan's excitement grew, and he meticulously planned the perfect proposal. Jhansi, adorned with twinkling lights and a hint of winter's enchantment, would provide the idyllic setting for this pivotal moment in their love story.

On the evening of December 24th, Ishan nervously awaited Varuni's arrival at their favourite spot in

Jhansi—a secluded bench nestled beneath a grand oak tree, its branches reaching toward the starlit sky.

Ishan: (heart pounding) "This is where it all begins."

When Varuni finally arrived, her eyes lit up with a curious sparkle as she took in the romantic atmosphere Ishan had created.

Varuni: (in awe) "Ishan, this is beautiful."

The soft glow of the lights reflected in her eyes, adding an ethereal touch to her beauty. With a deep breath, Ishan poured his heart out, expressing his love, admiration, and the depth of his feelings for her.

Ishan: (nervously) "Varuni, from the moment I saw you, my life changed. You're the missing piece to my puzzle, the melody to my song."

Varuni, her face adorned with a mixture of surprise and joy, listened intently to Ishan's heartfelt confession. Jhansi seemed to hold its breath, as if the very air hung in anticipation of her response. The world around them faded into insignificance, leaving only Ishan, Varuni, and the weight of their shared connection.

After a moment that felt like an eternity, Varuni's face broke into a radiant smile, her eyes shining with a warmth that mirrored Ishan's love.

Varuni: (teary-eyed) "Ishan, you've filled my life with happiness and love. I've fallen for you too."

With a voice filled with emotion, she reciprocated his feelings, confessing that she too had found solace and joy in his presence. Jhansi rejoiced in their newfound happiness, as if nature itself celebrated their union.

In that magical moment beneath the grand oak tree, Ishan and Varuni sealed their love with a tender embrace, their souls entwined in a promise of togetherness.

Ishan: (holding Varuni) "You've made me the happiest person alive."

Jhansi, with its timeless charm and whispered echoes, became a witness to their declaration, forever holding the echoes of their love story within its embrace.

As the night sky glittered with stars and the air filled with the music of their hearts, Ishan and Varuni embarked on a new journey—a journey of love, trust, and shared dreams.

Ishan: (looking at Varuni) "Our adventure begins now."

Jhansi, with its eternal beauty and tranquil charm, would forever hold a special place in their hearts, reminding them of the love that bloomed within its hallowed grounds.

Chapter 4

Embracing the Magic of "Salaam-e-Ishq"

With the arrival of the new year, Ishan and Varuni found themselves deeply immersed in the enchantment of their blossoming love. Jhansi, ever the silent observer, bore witness to their journey—a town that held the echoes of their laughter, the whispers of their dreams, and the tender moments that defined their romance.

One day, as they wandered through the heart of town, Ishan and Varuni stumbled upon the local cinema, its marquee adorned with posters announcing the screening of a romantic film titled "Salaam-e-Ishq." The very title resonated with their hearts, beckoning them to explore the magic of love as portrayed on the silver screen.

Ishan: (excited) "Varuni, have you heard about 'Salaam-e-Ishq'? It sounds incredible."

Varuni: (smiling) "I've heard great things. Let's go see it!"

Eager to experience the film's narrative, they purchased tickets and entered the theatre, filled with anticipation. The dimmed lights, the cozy atmosphere, and the scent of fresh popcorn in the air created an ambiance charged with excitement and the promise of a shared adventure.

As the film began, Ishan and Varuni found themselves transported into a world of love, passion, and the complexities of relationships. The story unfurled before them, weaving together the lives of various characters in a rich tapestry of emotions and destinies. They laughed at the witty banter, shed tears during the heart-wrenching moments, and held each other's hands tightly, their hearts resonating with the highs and lows of the characters' journeys.

"Salaam-e-Ishq" became more than just a movie—it became a reflection of Ishan and Varuni's own love story. They saw their hopes, fears, and dreams mirrored in the characters' experiences. The film spoke to the depth of their emotions, the intricacies of their connection, and the challenges they might face along the way.

As the final scenes played out and the credits began to roll, Ishan and Varuni exchanged a knowing glance, their hearts brimming with newfound understanding and affection. The film had touched their souls, leaving an indelible mark on their journey. Jhansi, with its timeless charm, seemed to embrace their love, offering a sanctuary where their hearts could soar.

From that day forward, Ishan and Varuni carried the spirit of "Salaam-e-Ishq" within their hearts. They understood that love was not simply an emotion portrayed on a screen—it was a vibrant tapestry woven through their own lives. Jhansi became the backdrop for their own real-life love story, a place where their hearts danced to the rhythm of their shared dreams and aspirations.

As their romance continued to unfold, Ishan and Varuni cherished each moment they spent together. They explored the hidden corners of Jhansi, hand in hand, allowing the magic of the town to infuse their relationship with wonder and joy. The echoes of their laughter filled the air, intertwining with the whispers of love that echoed through the town's quaint streets.

With every passing day, Ishan and Varuni discovered new depths of love and connection. Jhansi, with its enduring beauty and timeless charm, bore witness to their shared moments of tenderness, passion, and growth. It became a place where their love story was written, its pages filled with the sweet melodies of "Salaam-e-Ishq" that echoed in their hearts.

Chapter 5

A Twist of Fate

As April approached, Ishan found himself brimming with excitement over Varuni's upcoming birthday. Jhansi, adorned with blooming flowers and the gentle caress of spring, seemed to conspire in their Favor to make this celebration of their love truly special. Little did they suspect that this joyful anticipation would soon be eclipsed by an unforeseen twist of fate.

Ishan was determined to make Varuni's birthday unforgettable, and he meticulously planned the perfect gift. A day before her special day, they ventured into the local town's gift shop, hearts swelling with affection and the anticipation of the surprise that awaited her. Together, they roamed the store's aisles, on a quest to find a token of their love that could capture the depth of their connection.

As they immersed themselves in the task at hand, they remained blissfully unaware of an unseen presence nearby. In a town as close-knit as Jhansi, news had a way of spreading like wildfire. Little did Ishan and Varuni know that someone who had observed their tender moments had taken it upon themselves to meddle in their burgeoning romance.

While they were engrossed in their search for the perfect gift, Varuni's father received an anonymous call, informing him of his daughter's whereabouts—the local town market, in the company of someone he did not know. Shocked and concerned, Varuni's father felt compelled to intervene, oblivious to the depth of love that had blossomed between Ishan and Varuni.

He promptly called Varuni, urging her to return home without delay. Fearing the potential repercussions, she reluctantly agreed, promising her father that she would make her way back immediately. The weight of their love story hung heavily in the air, leaving both Ishan and Varuni with a sense of uncertainty and longing.

As hours turned into an agonizing night, Ishan anxiously awaited Varuni's call. The silence that enveloped his world seemed to reflect the void in his heart. Jhansi, with its timeless charm, offered no solace as Ishan's mind raced with thoughts of what had transpired. Each passing moment felt like an eternity, with questions and fears clouding his thoughts.

In the quiet of that night, Ishan's love for Varuni only intensified. He yearned to hear her voice, to reassure himself that their connection remained steadfast in the face of adversity. The moon cast its gentle glow upon him, as if offering a glimmer of hope in the darkness. Jhansi bore witness to his unwavering devotion, a testament to the depths of his love.

As dawn broke, Ishan's phone finally rang, and his heart skipped a beat when he saw Varuni's name on the screen. With trembling hands, he answered the call, relief washing over him as he heard her voice on the other end. The hours of uncertainty had come to an end, replaced by the reassurance that their love could withstand any storm.

Varuni explained the events that had unfolded—the intrusion into their love story and her father's concerns. Though her heart ached for the missed celebration, she reassured Ishan of her unwavering love. Jhansi, with its timeless charm, served as a reminder that their love was stronger than any obstacle.

In that moment, they silently vowed to weather the storms life might throw their way, to nurture their love and ensure its resilience. Jhansi became their sanctuary, offering solace and strength as Ishan and

Varuni navigated the complexities of their relationship.

As the sun rose over Jhansi, casting a warm, hopeful glow upon the town, Ishan and Varuni found solace in knowing that their love had emerged stronger from the trials they had faced. Their bond transcended the boundaries of distance and adversity, a testament to the depth of their connection.

And so, on Varuni's birthday, despite the physical separation, Ishan's heart remained entwined with hers. Jhansi, with its timeless charm, cradled their love within its embrace, offering hope for a future where their paths would converge once again.

Chapter 6

Paths Diverging

As days turned into weeks and their first year of college neared its end, Ishan and Varuni faced unexpected challenges that cast a shadow over their once-promising love story. The fateful night had left them with a lingering sense of uncertainty and a growing divide between them.

Varuni, feeling the weight of familial expectations and her own ambitions, reached out to Ishan to share a difficult decision. She explained that due to her commitment to preparing for her MBA, she had decided to join the Career Launcher Institute from the second year of college. This meant that their paths would diverge, and she would not be able to attend the remaining graduation classes with Ishan.

Ishan, taken aback and concerned by this sudden change, grappled with the implications of Varuni's decision. The dreams and aspirations they had built together seemed to hang in the balance, leaving him unsure of what the future held for their relationship.

Jhansi, with its timeless charm, provided the backdrop for their conversation, its gentle whispers carrying their hopes and fears. Ishan struggled to find the right words, torn between supporting Varuni's ambitions and yearning for their love to transcend the challenges before them.

Ishan: (worried) "Varuni, I understand your decision, but I'm scared. What will this mean for us? Can our love survive this distance?"

After a moment of silence, Ishan gathered his thoughts and continued, expressing his concerns and the depth of his love for Varuni. He shared his fears of growing apart, of losing the connection they had worked so hard to build. Jhansi bore witness to his vulnerability, offering a sense of solace amidst the uncertainty.

Varuni, on the other end of the line, empathized with Ishan's worries and shared his emotions. She, too, felt the pain of their impending separation and the weight of her future aspirations. In a tender and heartfelt tone, she reassured Ishan of her love and promised to make the most of the time they had together, cherishing each moment amidst their busy lives.

Varuni: (softly) "Ishan, our love is strong, and I believe in us. We'll make this work, and when we're reunited, our bond will be even stronger."

As the second year of college approached, Ishan and Varuni had to confront the reality of their diverging paths. Jhansi, with its timeless beauty, seemed to mourn their separation, mirroring their own complex emotions. The town that had witnessed the birth of their love story now stood witness to the challenges threatening to pull them apart.

During the exam period, Ishan and Varuni seized every opportunity to create cherished memories together, stealing precious hours between study sessions. Jhansi became their sanctuary, offering comfort and a reminder of the love they shared.

As days turned into months and seasons changed, Ishan and Varuni found themselves on separate journeys—Varuni focused on her MBA preparation at the Career Launcher Institute, while Ishan continued his studies at the local town college. Their lives became consumed by their individual pursuits, each day drawing them closer to their respective goals.

Jhansi, with its timeless charm, remained a constant presence in their hearts, a place where the memories of their love story lived on. Despite the physical distance, Ishan and Varuni drew strength from the love they shared, the echoes of their laughter, and the hope of a future where their paths might once again converge.

And so, as they navigated their separate journeys, Ishan and Varuni clung to the love that had brought them together. Jhansi, with its enduring beauty, served as a reminder of the bond they had forged—a bond that would endure the tests of time and distance.

Chapter 7

Challenges and Transitions

As weeks turned into months, Ishan and Varuni found themselves navigating the intricate dance of their evolving lives. Their paths had diverged, each now focused on individual aspirations and goals. Jhansi, with its enduring beauty, bore witness to the next chapter of their love story as it unfolded against a backdrop of new challenges.

Varuni's MBA preparations were in full swing, and she was gearing up to take on prestigious exams like CAT and XAT. Her unwavering commitment propelled her toward her ambitions, and she remained resolutely focused on her future objectives. Meanwhile, Ishan embarked on a journey of self-discovery, attending civil services classes following the completion of his college studies. He grappled with his own career aspirations, in search of a path that resonated with his passion and purpose.

Despite the physical distance and the introduction of new faces into their lives, Ishan and Varuni kept their daily phone conversations alive. They shared the minutiae of their routines, celebrated each other's triumphs, and leaned on one another during moments of struggle. Jhansi, an ever-present muse in their hearts, offered a comforting refuge where their souls could find solace amid life's challenges.

Their love, however, experienced its share of growth and uncertainty. As they pursued their individual journeys, the weight of their responsibilities and ambitions occasionally cast shadows over their relationship. The pressures and uncertainties of their futures strained their connection at times. Nevertheless, they clung to the love that had initially drawn them together, finding solace in moments of understanding and support.

With the onset of their third year, their trials became more pronounced. Varuni remained steadfast in her determination, guided by a clear vision of her future prospects that lent her a sense of purpose and direction. In contrast, Ishan continued to wrestle with his career aspirations, grappling with uncertainty while searching for clarity. Jhansi, timeless in its allure, seemed to reflect their inner turmoil, providing both comfort and a gentle reminder of the choices ahead.

As the year unfolded, Ishan and Varuni found themselves at a crossroads. Varuni's brother, who had already completed his MBA at a prestigious South Indian university, learned that her father, a government servant, was being transferred to a new city. This sudden development sent shockwaves through their lives, adding a new layer of complexity to their already challenging circumstances.

The looming separation weighed heavily on Ishan and Varuni, casting a shadow of uncertainty and heartache over their relationship. Jhansi, its beauty enduring, stood as a testament to the love they had shared, the memories they had crafted, and the resilience they had demonstrated thus far.

As their third year ended, Ishan and Varuni faced a pivotal moment in their relationship. They understood that tough decisions lay ahead, choices that would shape their future. Jhansi, with its timeless charm and the echoes of their shared memories, whispered encouragement, urging them to find the strength and courage to navigate the impending changes.

Chapter 8

A New Beginning

Varuni settled into her new life in the bustling city, embracing the challenges of a fresh start while carrying the memories of the love she had left behind. The pain of their parting still echoed in her heart, but the hope of their future together provided her with strength and determination.

Within a month, Varuni and her family had adapted to their new surroundings. She eagerly embraced the opportunities and experiences that awaited her while maintaining a constant connection with Ishan through daily conversations. In an era before the convenience of WhatsApp and other social media platforms, their relationship relied solely on phone calls and occasional letters, each message carrying the echoes of their love and longing.

With the announcement of their graduation results, Ishan and Varuni celebrated the culmination of their undergraduate journey. The question of their future loomed large, and their destinies were intricately linked to the choices they were about to make. Varuni's plan began to take shape, and she proposed the idea of both of them pursuing master's degrees at the same university in her hometown.

For Ishan, this decision meant leaving his hometown and his parents, a choice laden with challenges. As an only child, his parents understandably expressed concern and reluctance, but he managed to convince them, reassuring them that he would visit every weekend. With their blessings and encouragement, Ishan and Varuni enrolled at the same university, each selecting their respective courses—Varuni opting for an M. Com degree while Ishan pursued a master's in History, his chosen subject for civil services preparation.

The new city became their shared destination, a place where they could renew their dreams and aspirations together. Varuni stayed with her parents, and Ishan found accommodation in a nearby PG facility. Every morning, they embarked on their individual journeys, attending classes in different departments but united by the common goal of building a brighter future side by side.

The university environment was a novel experience for both Ishan and Varuni. During breaks, Varuni would zip over to Ishan on her scooter, and they would spend their free time chatting in the university canteen, sipping coffee, and sharing meals. It became their daily ritual—a cherished interlude amid the academic hustle and bustle.

As they adapted to their new surroundings, Ishan and Varuni consciously balanced their time between their own classmates and friends while cherishing their moments together. Their mutual understanding allowed them to respect each other's space and the need to connect with their peers.

However, as weeks stretched into months, the subtle growth of distance between them became noticeable. It was initially imperceptible, but it soon cast a shadow on their once-unbreakable bond. The demands of their respective courses and the allure of their individual social circles began to consume more of their time, leaving less room for the deep connection they had shared.

As they confronted fresh challenges and embarked on separate journeys within the same city, Ishan and Varuni found themselves at a crossroads once more. The future they had envisioned together now felt uncertain, and they both pondered if their love could endure the growing distance and the trials that lay ahead.

Jhansi, with its timeless charm, seemed to hold their shared memories and aspirations, gently reminding them of the love they once shared. The echoes of their laughter and the promise of a shared future still lingered in the tranquil air of the town, encouraging them to find a way to rekindle the spark that had brought them together.

Chapter 9

A Difficult Conversation

Ishan was in the midst of preparing for his classes when his phone suddenly rang. He picked it up, and on the other end, Varuni greeted him with a cheerful hello and asked him what he was up to. Ishan replied, "Just getting ready to meet you for class." Curiosity piqued; he inquired if everything was alright.

Varuni's response was tinged with a hint of uncertainty as she explained that she wouldn't be able to attend classes that day but promised to meet him during their break. Ishan, concerned, pressed gently, "Is everything okay?" Varuni reassured him, "We'll talk when we meet."

With those words, Ishan attended the first half of his classes at the university, eager to see Varuni during the break. His heart lifted at the thought of their meeting. He knew he loved her deeply, and he believed Varuni felt the same way. When she finally arrived on her scooter, her mere presence brought a smile to his face.

As they sat down together, a heavy silence hung between them, overshadowing the happiness Ishan had initially felt. Sensing that something significant was on Varuni's mind, he mustered the courage to break the silence. "Is everything okay?" he asked, concern etched on his face.

Varuni hesitated, her gaze shifting as she struggled to find the right words. After a prolonged pause, she finally began to speak. With a deep breath, she revealed her decision to drop her M. Com and CAT/MBA preparation. Instead, she had opted to pursue a career in Chartered Accountancy (CA) and had plans to move to Delhi for further preparation. She explained that Delhi had the best CA coaching centres, and her parents had agreed to her choice.

Ishan listened quietly, his emotions swirling within him as Varuni laid out her plans. His thoughts raced, and he wrestled with a mix of emotions. After her explanation, a heavy silence filled the air. He took a moment to process everything before speaking again.

"When are you leaving?" Ishan inquired softly, his voice tinged with uncertainty. "Can we still meet?" he asked, searching for some assurance in her eyes. Varuni met his gaze, but her silence spoke volumes. Ishan, feeling overwhelmed by the weight of her decision, abruptly got up from his seat and left for his PG accommodation without uttering another word.

Chapter 10

Confusion and Longing

Ishan returned to his place, his mind spinning from the heartfelt conversation with Varuni. The words they had exchanged left him in a state of bewilderment, unsure whether it was a real conversation or merely a dream. Lost in a whirlwind of thoughts, he eventually succumbed to fatigue, drifting off into a deep slumber.

Meanwhile, Varuni had retreated to her own home, but an unrelenting longing for Ishan compelled her to dial his number repeatedly since the afternoon. Their parting had been abrupt, and they hadn't had the chance for a final conversation. Varuni was on the cusp of embarking on a new journey to Delhi, carrying with her the weight of unspoken emotions, hoping for reconnection.

Days melted into nights, and Ishan's phone lay silent, buried under his deep slumber. Unaware of Varuni's persistent attempts to reach him, he finally stirred from his sleep in the late hours of the night. His heart skipped a beat as he discovered 125 missed calls from Varuni. Although it was well past midnight, Ishan didn't make an immediate effort to call her back, choosing instead to fall back into a fitful slumber.

The following morning brought a fresh attempt from Varuni to reach him. This time, Ishan answered the phone with a groggy voice, his senses still muddled by sleep. Irritation and concern-tinged Varuni's voice as she vented her frustration at Ishan's unavailability. His explanation of being asleep did not sit well with her, but she managed to convey her wish to meet him after the first half of the day. Ishan, his voice heavy with fatigue, agreed to the rendezvous.

Anticipation hung in the air as Varuni waited for Ishan at the campus canteen. She had dressed with care, donning a striking ensemble of denim and a new polo shirt, her hair elegantly tied up. Ishan's arrival brought a radiant smile to her face, and she wasted no time in suggesting they venture somewhere different from their usual canteen haunt.

Intrigued by her proposal, Ishan followed Varuni to her scooter, marvelling at her skilled manoeuvring through the streets. After a brief ride, they arrived at a local mall's parking lot. Varuni, her eyes sparkling with excitement, proposed watching a movie and then dropping Ishan back. While they secured tickets for the film "Welcome," featuring Katrina Kaif and Akshay Kumar, both knew that the movie was merely an excuse to spend more precious time together.

Throughout the screening, their hands were subtly intertwined, and their connection deepened with each passing moment. As the credits rolled and they exited the theatre, they found themselves in the newly opened McDonald's in town. The irresistible aroma of fast food filled the air as they sat together, savouring their McChicken burgers and cold drinks.

Amid bites of their meal, Varuni broke the silence that had settled between them by gently asking Ishan if there was something he wished to discuss after their recent conversation. Ishan, initially caught off guard, brushed off the idea, asserting that he was genuinely thrilled for Varuni's upcoming journey. He extended his congratulations and shared his own uncertainties regarding his future path, emphasizing his commitment to completing his post-graduation before making any definitive decisions.

With a complex blend of emotions, he presented Varuni with a carefully chosen gift—an elegant pearl bracelet symbolizing the depth of their bond. As he secured it around her wrist, tears welled up in Ishan's eyes, but words remained elusive. Varuni, equally moved, fought to keep her emotions in check, attempting to maintain her composure.

As the evening wore on, Ishan asked Varuni to drop him back at his PG. The ride back was marked by a heavy silence, both wrestling with their innermost thoughts, unspoken sentiments, and emotions simmering just beneath the surface. Upon reaching Ishan's PG, the reality of their impending separation weighed heavily on them.

Varuni revealed that her departure for Delhi was imminent, scheduled for the next day. The night was still, their shared silence echoing the weight of unspoken goodbyes, leaving them with a lingering sense of longing as they bade each other farewell for the night.

Chapter 11

The Departure

The morning sun cast a golden hue over, painting a picturesque scene that seemed at odds with the turmoil in Ishan and Varuni's hearts. With heavy hearts, they faced the day of Varuni's departure for Delhi. It was a day they had both been dreading, a day that marked a new chapter in their lives—one filled with uncertainty and longing.

Ishan had barely slept the night before, his mind filled with thoughts of Varuni and the impending separation. He had spent the restless hours going over their time together, cherishing every memory they had created, and silently wrestling with his own emotions. It was a battle between his love for Varuni and the desire to see her succeed in her chosen path.

Meanwhile, Varuni had spent her final night in quiet contemplation. She had packed her belongings, leaving behind the room that held echoes of their shared moments. Each item she placed in her suitcase felt like a piece of their love story, and the weight of it all settled deep within her heart.

The hours leading up to Varuni's departure were filled with a solemn sense of inevitability. Ishan helped her load her luggage into her father's car, their interactions marked by a heavy silence. The love they had once openly expressed now hung in the air unspoken, its presence felt in every lingering glance and hesitant touch.

**Ishan: ** (voice heavy) Are you sure about this, Varuni?

**Varuni: ** (teary-eyed) I must do this, Ishan. It is an opportunity I cannot let go of. But it does not mean... it does not mean I want to go.

**Ishan: ** (softly) I know, and I want you to succeed, Varuni. But it's just... it's hard, you know?

**Varuni: ** (nodding) I understand, Ishan. This is hard for me too. But I promise, we'll make it work. Our love is stronger than any distance.

As they stood by the car, Varuni's father, aware of the depth of their connection, gave Ishan a reassuring nod, silently acknowledging the bond between him and his daughter. It was a gesture that spoke volumes, a testament to the respect and affection they had for each other.

**Varuni's Father: ** (gruffly) Take care of yourself, Ishan. Look after her, even from afar.

**Ishan: ** (earnestly) I will, sir. You have my word.

With a final embrace that held the promise of a future reunion, Varuni reluctantly tore herself away from Ishan's arms. Her eyes glistened with unshed tears, mirroring the ache in Ishan's heart. She entered the car, her gaze locked with his until the very last moment when the vehicle drove away, taking her farther from Jhansi and from him.

Ishan watched the car until it disappeared from view, his heart heavy with the weight of their separation. The town, with its timeless charm, seemed to mourn the loss of their love story, the echoes of their laughter fading into the distance. The realization that he would no longer see Varuni on a daily basis hit him like a wave of loneliness, and he knew that life would never be the same.

In the days that followed, Ishan tried to fill the void left by Varuni's absence. He attended his classes, met with friends, and pursued his studies with determination. But no matter how occupied he kept himself, he couldn't escape the ache in his heart and the longing for the person who had become an integral part of his life.

**Ishan: ** (whispering to himself) Varuni, I miss you so much.

city, with its enduring beauty and timeless charm, served as a constant reminder of their love story. Each corner of the town held memories of their time together, and every whisper of the wind seemed to carry Varuni's name. The town had witnessed the evolution of their relationship—from silent admiration to profound love—and it held their shared moments in its embrace.

As the days turned into weeks and weeks into months, Ishan and Varuni continued to stay in touch through phone calls and messages. Their conversations were filled with updates about their lives and dreams, yet the underlying current of longing remained unspoken. They both knew that distance had come between them, but the bond they shared refused to wane.

**Varuni: ** (voice cracking) Ishan, I miss you more than words can say.

Despite the physical separation, Ishan and Varuni clung to the love that had brought them together. They remained committed to their individual pursuits, nurturing their dreams while cherishing the shared promise of a future where their paths might converge once again.

**Ishan: ** (softly, to himself) One day, Varuni, we will find our way back to each other.

And so, city, with its timeless charm and the whispers of their love story, held their memories close, a silent witness to the enduring connection that transcended the miles between them. The town, which had once celebrated their love, now stood as a beacon of hope, reminding them that their story was far from over.

Chapter 12

Navigating New Beginnings

Months had passed since Varuni's departure to Delhi. The seasons changed, and with them, the landscape of city transformed. Ishan had continued his studies, focusing on his master's degree while still preparing for the civil services exams. His life had taken on a routine that helped keep the ache of Varuni's absence at bay.

Varuni, on the other hand, had settled into the bustling life of Delhi. Her days were filled with intensive CA classes, and she had adapted to the fast-paced rhythm of the city. Despite the demands of her new life, thoughts of Ishan continued to occupy a special place in her heart.

One evening, after a long day of classes and revision, Varuni decided to take a break and visit a nearby park. As she strolled along the winding paths, the memories of Jhansi flooded her mind. She missed the tranquillity of the town, the gentle rustle of leaves, and the echoes of their love.

**Varuni: ** (softly to herself) Jhansi... Ishan...

She reached for her phone, contemplating calling Ishan to hear his voice and share her day. It had become a routine for them to exchange stories about their lives, bridging the distance with their words. But she hesitated. A nagging feeling of guilt and concern held her back.

**Varuni: ** (whispering) I don't want to disrupt his studies. He has his exams coming up.

Meanwhile, at his PG, Ishan sat at his desk, engrossed in his textbooks. The weight of his academic responsibilities bore down on him, and he had been diligently sticking to his study schedule. However, the silence of the room seemed to amplify his loneliness.

**Ishan: ** (sighing) I wish Varuni were here. Her presence always brightened my day.

Just as he muttered those words, his phone lit up with a message from Varuni. It was as if their thoughts had connected across the miles.

**Varuni's Message: ** (typing) Hey, Ishan. How's your day going?

Ishan's face broke into a warm smile as he read her message. He quickly typed a response.

**Ishan: ** (typing) Hey, Varuni! My day was okay. How about yours?

**Varuni's Message: ** (typing) It was hectic as usual, but I'm getting used to the Delhi rush. (pauses) I miss you.

Ishan's heart skipped a beat at those words. He typed his reply with genuine affection.

**Ishan: ** (typing) I miss you too, Varuni. Every day.

Their conversation continued, flowing effortlessly as they shared the ups and downs of their lives. Varuni told Ishan about her progress in her CA classes, and he updated her on his studies and preparations. The connection between them, even though the screen, was undeniable.

**Varuni's Message: ** (typing) Ishan, there is something I want to tell you.

**Ishan: ** (typing) What is it, Varuni?

**Varuni's Message: ** (typing) I have been thinking a lot about us and our future. I can't stop thinking about you, Ishan.

Ishan's heart raced as he read her message. His fingers trembled as he typed his response.

**Ishan: ** (typing) Varuni, I have been thinking about us too. I love you so much.

**Varuni's Message: ** (typing) I love you too, Ishan. And I want to be with you, more than anything.

Their words hung in the air, a declaration of love that transcended the distance between them. As the evening sun dipped below the horizon, casting a warm glow over Jhansi and the bustling streets of Delhi, Ishan and Varuni found solace in knowing that their love remained unwavering. It was a new beginning, a rekindling of their shared dreams, and the promise of a future where their paths would once again converge.

**Ishan: ** (whispering) Varuni, I will do whatever it takes to be with you.

**Varuni: ** (softly) And I will do the same, Ishan. Our love will guide us.

As they continued their conversation, their hearts felt lighter, and the burden of distance seemed to fade away. Jhansi, with its enduring charm and whispered echoes, held their hopes and dreams, a silent witness to the enduring love story that had captured their hearts.

**Ishan: ** (smiling) Our love story is not over, Varuni. It's just taking a new turn.

**Varuni: ** (with hope) Yes, Ishan. A new beginning for us.

And so, as the night settled over Jhansi and the bustling city of Delhi, Ishan and Varuni embraced the promise of their renewed love. The future held challenges, but their bond was unbreakable. They knew that together; they could navigate any obstacle and create a path that would lead them back to each other's arms.

Chapter 13

A Bold Decision

Ishan and Varuni's renewed connection brought a newfound sense of purpose to their lives. Days turned into weeks, and their conversations grew more intimate, filled with dreams and plans for their future together. The time apart had only strengthened their bond, and they were determined to bridge the distance that separated them.

One crisp evening, while Ishan sat by his window, gazing at the serene landscape of city, he received a video call from Varuni. Her face lit up his screen, and he couldn't help but smile.

**Varuni: ** (grinning) Hey there, handsome.

**Ishan: ** (smiling) Hey, beautiful. How's Delhi treating you today?

**Varuni: ** (sighs) It's the same old hustle and bustle, but it's different now.

**Ishan: ** (curious) What do you mean?

**Varuni: ** (pauses) Ishan, remember how we used to talk about our dreams, our future together?

**Ishan: ** (nodding) Of course, Varuni. It's what kept us going.

**Varuni: ** (determined) Well, I have been thinking. What if we stop talking about it and start making it happen?

Ishan's eyes widened in surprise. He had an inkling of what Varuni was implying, but he wanted to hear it from her.

**Ishan: ** (encouraging) Go on, Varuni. What are you thinking?

**Varuni: ** (takes a deep breath) Ishan, what if I move back to you?

Ishan's heart skipped a beat. The idea of Varuni returning to their hometown filled him with excitement, but he wanted to ensure it was the right decision for her.

**Ishan: ** (thoughtful) Varuni, that would be incredible, but what about your CA studies and your plans in Delhi?

**Varuni: ** (determined) Ishan, I have thought about it long and hard. I can continue my CA studies here. There are coaching centres here too. And as for my parents, they have agreed to support my decision if it's what I really want.

**Ishan: ** (moved) Varuni, you are willing to make this sacrifice for us?

**Varuni: ** (smiling) It is not a sacrifice, Ishan. It's a choice I'm making because I want to be with you more than anything else in this world.

Tears welled up in Ishan's eyes as he realized the depth of Varuni's love and commitment.

**Ishan: ** (emotional) Varuni, you have no idea how much this means to me. I love you so much, and having you here with me would be a dream come true.

**Varuni: ** (teary-eyed) I love you too, Ishan. More than words can express.

With their hearts intertwined and a shared dream of building a life together in city, Ishan and Varuni made a bold decision that would change the course of their lives. They were determined to face the challenges that lay ahead, to nurture their love, and to create a future filled with happiness and shared dreams.

Over the next few months, Varuni wrapped up her commitments in Delhi and prepared for her move back to Jhansi. She found a suitable coaching centre for her CA studies and ensured that her parents were supportive of her decision. Ishan, in turn, continued his studies with a renewed sense of purpose, eagerly awaiting Varuni's return.

city, with its timeless charm, seemed to celebrate their decision, as if nature itself rejoiced in the reunion of two souls deeply in love. The town that had witnessed their love story from its inception now stood witness to a new chapter, a chapter filled with hope, determination, and the promise of a shared future.

As they counted down the days until Varuni's return, Ishan and Varuni knew that their love story was far from over. It was evolving into something even more beautiful—a story of courage, commitment, and the enduring power of love.

Chapter 14

Uncertain Paths

As Varuni wrapped up her life in Delhi, preparing to return to Ishan, unexpected opportunities knocked on her door. She received an offer to work with a prestigious CA firm in Delhi itself, aligning perfectly with her ongoing studies. This twist of fate threw her plans into disarray, causing her to reconsider her path. Meanwhile, Ishan had completed his master's degree and was gearing up for his civil services preparations, a significant milestone in his journey.

In their conversations over the phone, amidst the excitement of reuniting, they found themselves grappling with conflicting desires. Varuni shared her dilemma with Ishan, and amidst their discussions, a new plan emerged. Varuni suggested that Ishan move to Delhi to explore better opportunities, allowing them to be together while she pursued her career and studies. Both embraced this decision, hoping for a smoother path ahead.

Ishan promptly relocated to Delhi, securing admission to Vajiram and Ravi for his civil services preparation. Varuni, on the other hand, embarked on her internship at the CA firm, reveling in their reunions every weekend. However, as they delved deeper into their respective pursuits, life began to unfold in unexpected ways.

Amidst the rhythm of their lives, Varuni received an enticing offer from a firm in Chennai. The prospect of a lucrative position coupled with the opportunity to continue her CA preparations and pursue her law studies simultaneously intrigued her. She shared this news with Ishan, who initially grappled with disappointment. Yet, as they discussed further, they realized the importance of seizing opportunities, even if it meant being physically apart for a while.

With a heavy heart, they agreed to the new plan: Varuni would relocate to Chennai for a year to pursue this opportunity, with the hope of reuniting stronger than ever. Little did they know, the journey ahead would test their resolve and challenge their relationship in unforeseen ways. Yet, amidst the uncertainty, they held onto the belief that their love would endure, guiding them through the tumultuous paths that lay ahead.

Chapter 15

Distance and Determination

As Varuni embarked on her journey to Chennai, bidding a temporary farewell to Ishan, the weight of their separation hung heavy in their hearts. The bustling streets of the new city and the unfamiliar faces only accentuated their longing for each other. Despite the physical distance, they remained connected through late-night calls, text messages filled with words of encouragement, and the promise of a future together.

In Chennai, Varuni threw herself into her work with fervour, immersing herself in the challenges and opportunities that lay ahead. Each day brought new lessons and experiences, yet her thoughts often drifted back to Ishan, his unwavering support serving as a beacon of hope during uncertainty.

Meanwhile, Ishan delved deeper into his civil services preparations in Delhi, finding solace in the routine of his studies yet longing for Varuni's presence by his side. The weekends, once filled with laughter and shared moments, now felt empty without her. Yet, amidst the solitude, he found strength in their shared dreams and the promise of a future where they would no longer be separated by miles.

As months passed, both Varuni and Ishan encountered obstacles along their respective paths. Varuni faced the challenges of adapting to a new environment, navigating office politics, and balancing her studies with her professional responsibilities. Ishan, too, grappled with the demands of his rigorous preparation, moments of self-doubt creeping in amidst the pressure to succeed.

Yet, through it all, their love remained unwavering, a source of comfort and inspiration in times of uncertainty. They drew strength from each other, celebrating small victories and offering solace during moments of despair. And as they continued to navigate the trials and tribulations of distance, their determination to overcome obstacles only grew stronger, fuelling their belief in a future where they would finally be together once more.

Chapter 16

Bridges Across Distance

The bond between Varuni and Ishan, once solidified by shared dreams and unyielding love, now faced the ultimate test: the trial of distance. As Varuni navigated the bustling streets of Chennai and Ishan immersed himself in the chaotic rhythm of Delhi, the miles between them seemed to stretch infinitely, casting shadows of doubt and uncertainty upon their once unwavering connection.

The challenges of a long-distance relationship began to manifest, casting a pall over their once vibrant love. The absence of physical presence weighed heavily on their hearts, leaving them longing for the warmth of each other's embrace. The late-night calls and text messages, once a source of comfort, now served as painful reminders of the chasm that separated them.

Miscommunication became an all-too-common occurrence, as words spoken through screens failed to convey the depth of their emotions. Insecurities festered in the silence between conversations, doubts creeping in like shadows in the night. And amidst the chaos of their individual lives, the distance threatened to erode the foundation of their once unbreakable bond.

Yet, amidst the turmoil, Varuni and Ishan refused to surrender to despair. They fought tirelessly to bridge the gap between them, weaving strands of hope and determination into the fabric of their relationship. They scheduled virtual dates, pouring their hearts out across video calls and sharing the minutiae of their daily lives to remain connected.

But even as they struggled to maintain their connection, external pressures threatened to tear them apart. Varuni's demanding job and Ishan's intensive studies left little room for compromise, leaving them both feeling overwhelmed and exhausted. Conflicts arose, fuelled by the frustrations of distance and the weight of their individual burdens.

Yet, in the midst of their struggles, Varuni and Ishan found solace in the memories of their shared past and the promise of a future together. They clung to the belief that their love was worth fighting for, a beacon of hope amidst the darkness that threatened to engulf them.

And so, with hearts heavy yet spirits unbroken, Varuni and Ishan vowed to weather the storms that lay ahead, knowing that with patience, understanding, and unwavering devotion, they could overcome the trials of distance and emerge stronger than ever before.

Chapter 17

Burdens of Duty

To divert their minds Ishan's decision to pursue higher education and his preparations for the JNU entrance exam, while Varuni continues her internship. This sets the stage for the sudden twist in Ishan's life when he receives a call from his father about his mother's accident and subsequent diagnosis of mouth cancer.

Ishan immediately puts his own plans on hold and rushes back to his hometown to be with his family, informing Varuni and his classes about the situation. Despite the distance, Varuni remains supportive and stays connected with Ishan over the phone, showing her concern and helping.

Upon returning home, Ishan takes on the role of caregiver for his parents, particularly his mother who is undergoing medical treatment. This highlights Ishan's sense of duty and responsibility as the only child in the family, and the emotional toll it takes on him.

As Ishan's mother's condition worsens with the diagnosis of mouth cancer, Ishan and his family are faced with uncertainty and fear. Varuni also becomes involved, offering suggestions and support from afar. The sudden turn of events leaves Ishan feeling lonely and tense, unable to focus on his own plans and studies.

With the decision to take Ishan's mother to Kolkata for surgery, Ishan is fully involved in the process, supporting his family every step of the way. Varuni, although supportive, is also preoccupied with her own responsibilities, leading to a decrease in communication between her and Ishan.

Despite their initial strong connection, the strain of the crisis and the demands of their individual lives cause a noticeable decrease in communication between Ishan and Varuni. Both are left wondering about the reasons behind this change, but the pressing nature of Ishan's family situation leaves little room for them to address it directly.

Deep into the complexities of family dynamics and the strain it can put on relationships. It highlights Ishan and Varuni's struggles to navigate their personal and familial responsibilities while maintaining their connection amidst a challenging time.

Chapter 18

The Silent Pain

Months had passed since Ishan's mother underwent surgery, but instead of recovery, her health had only deteriorated as cancer spread relentlessly throughout her body. The inevitable happened five months post-surgery, leaving Ishan and his father shattered. It was an early morning when Ishan's mother took her last breath, leaving behind an irreplaceable void in their lives.

Ishan found himself grappling with the shock of her sudden departure, seeking solace in the routine of funeral rituals and mourning. Throughout the process, he clung to his father, finding strength in their shared grief. But amidst the condolences and prayers of friends and family, one absence weighed heavily on Ishan's heart – Varuni's.

Despite numerous attempts to reach out, Varuni remained conspicuously silent, adding to Ishan's anguish. He longed to hear her voice, to feel her support during this trying time, yet her absence only amplified his sense of isolation.

As the days passed, Ishan's phone finally rang, and it was Varuni on the other end. The conversation hung heavy with unspoken words and unresolved emotions. Ishan struggled to find his voice amidst the flood of thoughts and feelings, while Varuni seemed oblivious to his silent pain.

She spoke of her busy schedule and mundane details, unaware of the gaping void in Ishan's world. He listened, feeling the chasm between them widen with each passing moment. In that silence, Ishan realized the depth of his solitude, longing for a connection that seemed lost amidst the noise of life.

This marked a pivotal moment in Ishan's journey, a silent confrontation with the absence of solace when it was needed the most. It was a chapter of silent pain, where words failed to bridge the divide between two hearts drifting apart amidst the tumult of loss and longing.

Chapter 19

The Silent Break

In the aftermath of their shared loss, the once inseparable bond between Ishan and Varuni had gradually eroded into a silent chasm. Despite the palpable tension and unspoken words, neither could fathom the reason behind their sudden estrangement.

Days turned into weeks, with Ishan immersed in memories of his childhood and uncertain about his future, while Varuni navigated her busy schedule with a heavy heart. The silence between them echoed louder than any spoken word, noticed even by their friends and acquaintances who sensed the distance growing between the two lovers.

After a month of agonizing silence, one afternoon, Ishan's phone broke the stillness, and Varuni's name flashed across the screen. A glimmer of hope flickered in Ishan's eyes as he answered the call, but it was quickly extinguished by Varuni's cold tone.

"Hi," she said tersely, devoid of the warmth that once filled their conversations. Ishan replied in kind, masking his inner turmoil with forced composure. Varuni wasted no time in getting to the point, expressing her decision with a finality that left Ishan reeling.

She explained that it was better for both of them to sever ties, to cease all communication without explanation or remorse. And just like that, with a few words, the lifeline that had sustained them for seven years was abruptly cut.

Ishan stood frozen, the weight of Varuni's words crashing down upon him like a tidal wave. He held onto the phone, unable to comprehend the suddenness of their demise, grappling with the reality of their shattered dreams.

Barely a month had passed since Ishan bid farewell to his mother, and now, he found himself mourning yet another loss – the loss of love, the loss of connection, the loss of the future he had envisioned with Varuni.

marked the culmination of their silent descent into heartbreak, a stark reminder of the fragility of love and the devastating consequences of unspoken words. It was a chapter of grief and acceptance, as Ishan came to terms with the irrevocable end of a love that once defined his world.

Epilogue

Echoes of Silence

In the wake of Ishan and Varuni's abrupt separation, life moved on, albeit with a lingering sense of emptiness for both. Days turned into weeks, and weeks into months, yet the echoes of their silent break reverberated in the depths of their souls.

Ishan sought solace in the familiar routines of his home, finding comfort in the memories of his mother and the unconditional love of his father. Though the pain of loss still gnawed at his heart, he embraced each day with renewed determination, determined to forge a path forward despite the scars left by love's betrayal.

Varuni, too, navigated life's tumultuous waters with a steely resolve, burying her emotions beneath a facade of indifference. Yet, in the quiet moments of solitude, she could not escape the haunting spectre of what could have been, haunted by the ghost of a love lost to the silence of unspoken truths.

Time marched on, softening the sharp edges of their pain, and granting them the gift of perspective. As seasons changed and wounds healed, Ishan and Varuni found themselves on separate journeys of self-discovery, each carving out a new identity forged in the crucible of their shared past.

Though their paths diverged, the bond they once shared remained etched in the fabric of their beings, a bittersweet reminder of love's enduring legacy. And as they moved forward, carrying the weight of their silent past, they found solace in the knowledge that sometimes, in the quiet spaces between heartbreak and healing, true redemption lies waiting to be found.

The epilogue served as a poignant conclusion to Ishan and Varuni's story, offering a glimpse into their lives beyond the tumult of their shared past. It was a testament to the resilience of the human spirit, as they embraced the complexities of love and loss, finding strength in the echoes of silence that bound them together, even in their darkest hour.

Reflecting on the events that transpired, it indeed seemed as though Ishan may have sensed the impending finality of their last phone call. Perhaps his intuition whispered warnings of the impending break, though he may not have fully comprehended its gravity at the time. As for Varuni, her motivations and intentions remained shrouded in ambiguity, leaving Ishan to grapple with unanswered questions and unresolved emotions.

In the aftermath of their separation, both Ishan and Varuni embarked on separate journeys, each navigating the labyrinth of life's uncertainties in their own way. Their paths diverged, leading them to unfamiliar territories devoid of the shared comfort they once found in each other's presence.

Despite the absence of communication or contact, the imprint of their love lingered, a faint echo of what once was. Yet, as time passed and life carried on, they drifted further apart, losing touch with mutual friends and fading into the backdrop of each other's memories.

In retrospect, it seemed as though their meeting in this life had served a purpose – to experience and share a profound bond of love and companionship. And once that purpose was fulfilled, they were destined to part ways, their paths intertwining briefly before diverging once more.

As they navigated the ebb and flow of life's currents, Ishan and Varuni found solace in the knowledge that their time together, however fleeting, had left an indelible mark on their souls. And though they may never cross paths again, the love they shared would forever remain a cherished chapter in the story of their lives.

Hope one day they forgive each other for not being what they wanted each other to be

****